EXCUSE ME!

by Lisa Kopelke

SIMON & SCHUSTER BOOKS FOR YOUNG READERS
NEW YORK LONDON TORONTO SYDNEY SINGAPORE

SIMON & SCHUSTER BOOKS FOR YOUNG READERS
An imprint of Simon & Schuster Children's Publishing Division
1230 Avenue of the Americas, New York, New York 10020

Book design by Greg Stadnyk
The text for this book is set in Green and Neo Neo.
The illustrations for this book are rendered in acrylic.
Manufactured in China
4 6 8 10 9 7 5
Library of Congress Cataloging-in-Publication Data
Kopelke, Lisa.
Excuse me! / Lisa Kopelke.
p. cm.
Summary: A frog who loves to burp learns the value of good manners.
ISBN 0-689-85111-1
[1. Frogs—Fiction. 2. Belching—Fiction. 3. Behavior.] I. Title.
PZ7.K83614 Ex 2003
[Fic]—dc21 2002001261

To Clairice

• SPECIAL THANKS •
Mom & Dad
Irma Lindley
Chris Mortenson
Steven Malk
David Gale
Greg Stadnyk
Mary Sue Milliken
Susan Feniger
Lisa Wheeler
Janie Bynum

Frog loved to eat.

And Frog loved to burp.

·FROG·

When Frog was just a tadpole, he ate a lot and burped freely.

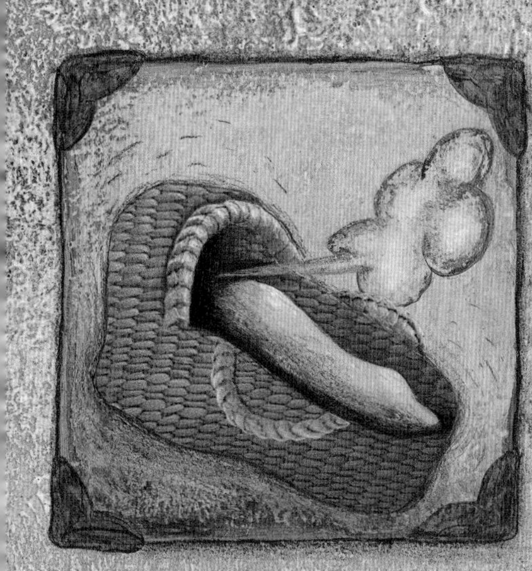

The Great Annual Frog Jam • Flypie-eating contest •
1st
PLACE

Wherever he went, townsfolk would comment.

"What a good eater!"

"Oh, how cute!"

"Just like his father!" they said.

As Frog grew, so did his appetite. He ate more and he burped more.

And Frog ate everything.

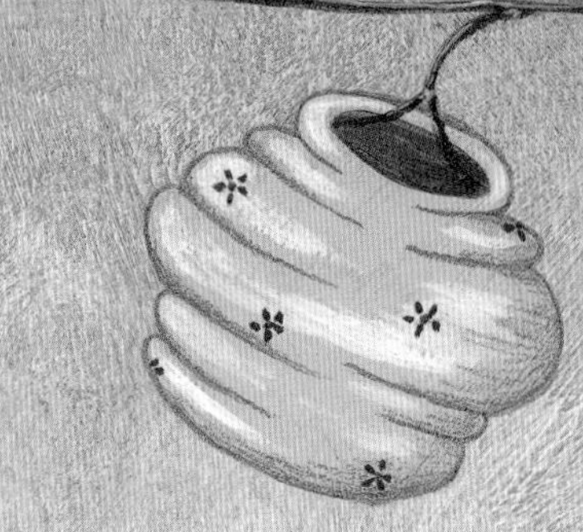

He snacked on fly noodles and cricket tacos. He gulped down worm burgers and dragonfly soup.

"Enthusiastic burping," thought Frog,
"not only feels good, but also
makes room for dessert!"

As Frog got older he began to notice that not everyone appreciated his burping as much as he did.

At first, they held napkins up to their faces and looked away.

"Ahem!" folks said.

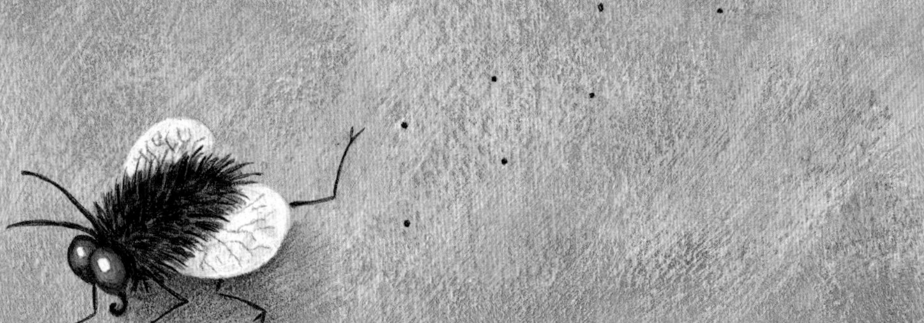

One time, after a delicious dinner and a huge burp, Frog's friends actually got up from the table and left.

"YUCK!" they cried as they all stormed out the door.

Agenda: BURPING!

(gassamous-expellerous-grossamus)

MAYOR

Finally the townsfolk reached their limit. Mr. Mayor called a meeting.

"Something has to be done!" he said.

They took a vote and decided to send Frog up the river.

#1

Frog was sad and confused. He packed a big lunch, waved good-bye, and left for his journey.

Along the way Frog grew hungry and he stopped to eat.

After a tasty meal, a loud burp, and a long nap, Frog awoke to a faint, familiar sound in the distance. Curious, he followed the sound. As Frog got closer, he realized it was the sound of burping.

Happy, beautiful burping!

He wandered into the town and saw new frogs of all shapes, sizes, and colors eating and burping freely.

Frog was excited.

The new frogs welcomed him with open arms and stinky burps.

Frog jumped right in.

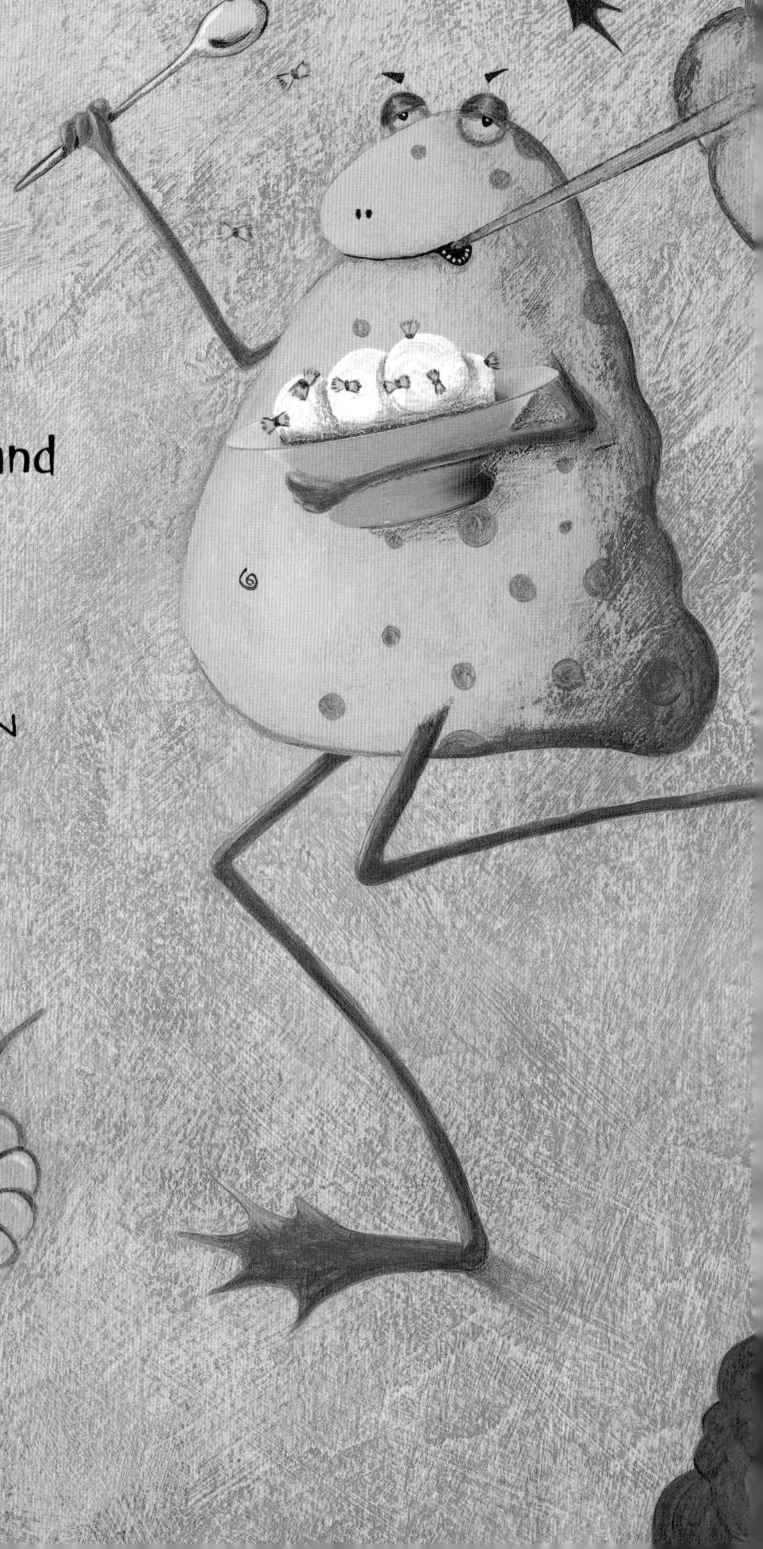

They dined on centipede soufflés and ladybug stew.

"Burp!"

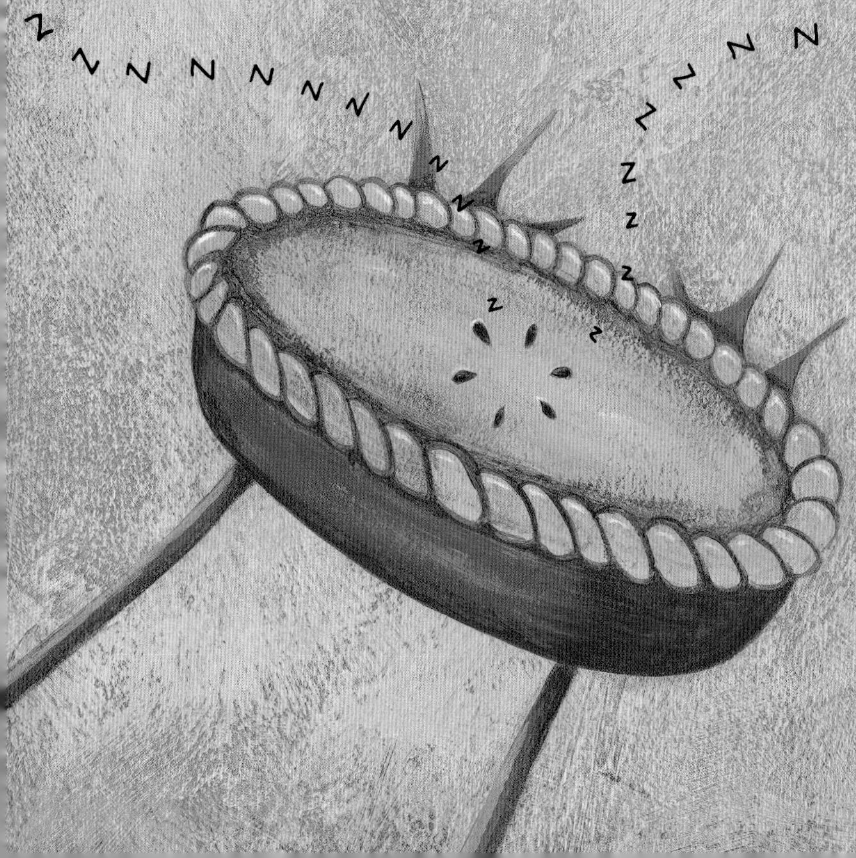

They devoured mosquito pies and moths à la mode.

"Buhrrraaap!"

The frogs burped all day.

The frogs burped all night.

The frogs even burped while they slept.

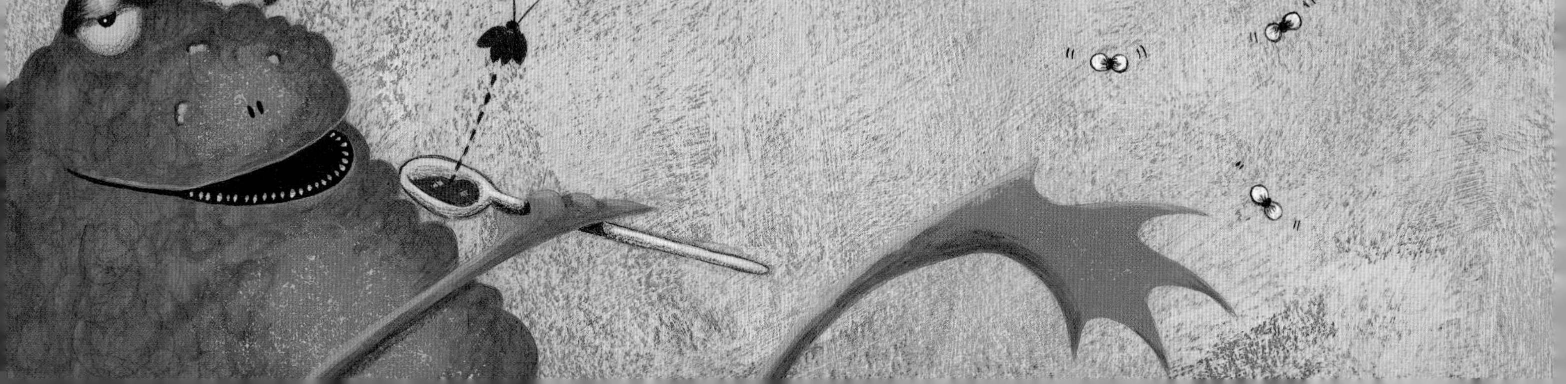

Frog was thrilled to
be eating and burping
with his new friends, but
he soon discovered that they
never stopped burping, and they never
said excuse me.

Frog became disgusted.

One day Frog was sitting in the café, eating and trying to keep his burps to himself, when he saw a flyer on the wall for the Great Annual Frog Jam in his hometown.

It was Frog's favorite event. Frog decided he had to go home.

Nervous that he would not be welcome, he wore a disguise.

At the Frog Jam, things were hopping. The smell of exotic foods filled the air. Frog's mouth watered in anticipation as he strolled over to the food stands. A crowd was gathered around his favorite, Three-Beetle Chili. Mr. Mayor, Mrs. Mayor, and Baby Mayor were slurping it down by the gallons. Frog joined in and ate so much, so fast, that a large burp almost escaped. Frog tried to hold it back.

But then, Baby Mayor let
out a gigantic burp.

"Excuse me!"
he said in a small voice.

One by one the crowd struck up a chorus of burps. They couldn't help it. Even Mr. Mayor and Mrs. Mayor were burping. A Three-Beetle-Chili cloud hung in the air.

"Excuse me!" they all cried.

Frog could not keep it down any longer.

"BUHRRR

The burp was so big his disguise flew off!

The crowd gasped.

RRRAAAAAAAP!"

"Um, excuse me!" said Frog.

"Frog," Mr. Mayor declared,
"you are excused!"

The townsfolk cheered. They were glad to have Frog back, and Frog was happy to finally be home.

Frog still loved to eat.

And Frog still loved to burp.

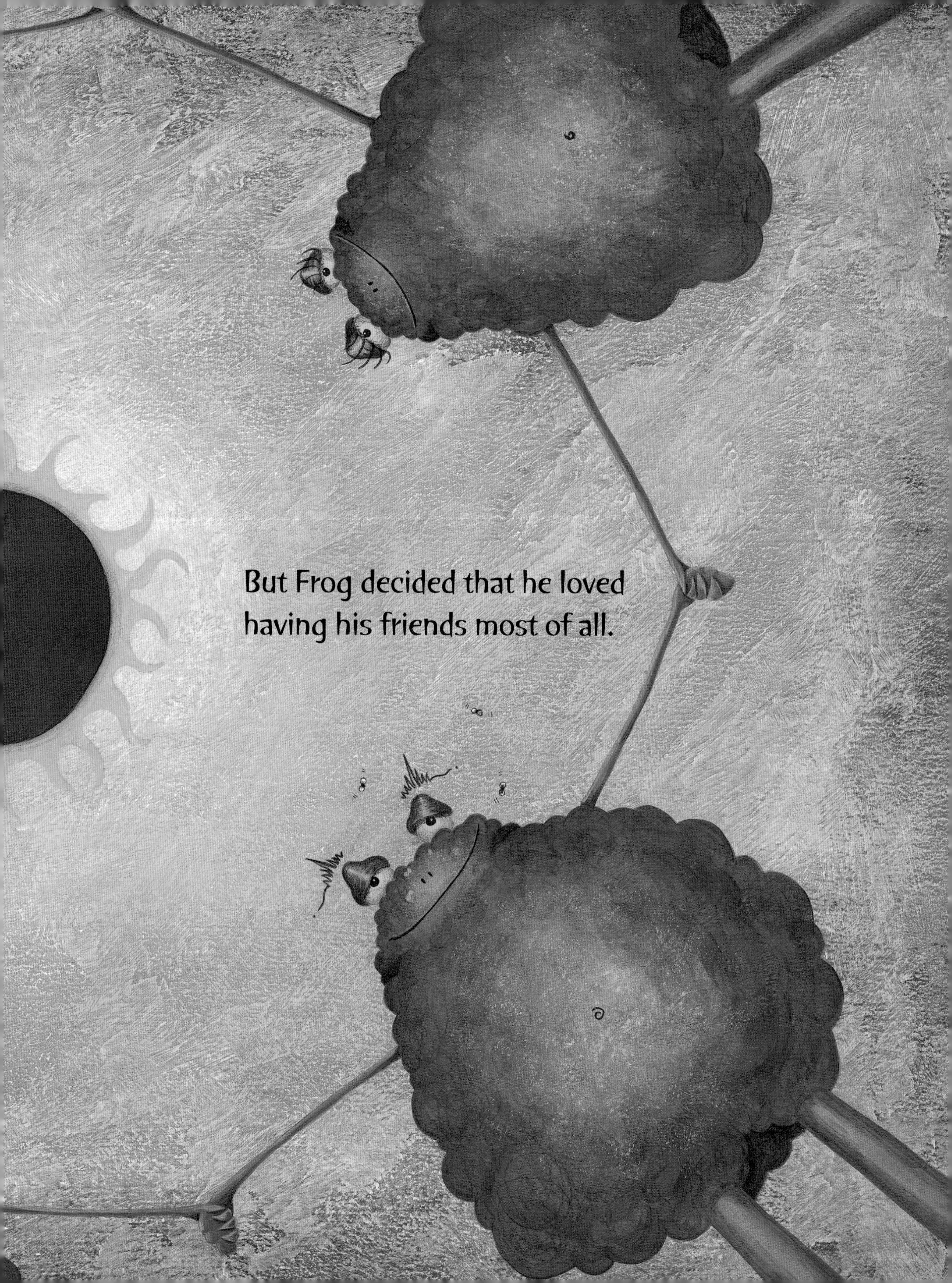

But Frog decided that he loved
having his friends most of all.

"BURP!"

"Excuse me!"